*For Anita*

First published in the U.S. in 1989
by Ideals Publishing Corporation,
Nashville, TN 37214

Originally published in 1989 in Great Britain
by Walker Books Ltd., London

Text copyright ©1989 by Dennis Reader
Illustrations copyright ©1989 by Dennis Reader

Printed in Hong Kong by South China Printing Co.

ISBN 0-8249-8386-6

# A Lovely Bunch of COCONUTS

## Dennis Reader

**IDEALS CHILDREN'S BOOKS**
**Nashville, Tennessee**

Once, on a little island shaded by a single coconut palm, there lived a happy man.

Across the water lived a greedy king who was always looking at the little island through his binoculars.

The king wanted the man's little island for himself.

"Why do you want his little island?" asked the queen.
"Because I want that lovely bunch of coconuts,"
 said the king.
"That's all he's got," said the queen.
"That's all I want," said the king.

The more the king stared at the little island,
the more he wanted it.

And the man on the little island stared back at the king and wondered.

One day the king took action. He summoned his champion Olympic swimmer, his head gardener, his pet vulture, his cousin the pole vaulter, and the palace cook.

"I want that island," said the king.

"One of you must get it for me."

He pointed to the swimmer. "You first."

And still the happy man watched and wondered.

The champion Olympic swimmer didn't
really want to go, but the king's word was
law, and so he dived into the water.
"I'm coming to get you!" he shouted.

But when he reached the
little island, the man hit
him with a coconut.
The Olympic champion
swam back with a bump on
his head and set off at once for the desert.

Next, the king ordered his head gardener to tunnel under the seabed.
The gardener kept a nice straight line and came up on the little island.

The man hit him with
a coconut.
The gardener tunneled
back and got on with some
urgent work in his greenhouse.

But the king had plenty more tricks up his sleeve.

He signaled to his pet vulture.

"Go get him!" he cried.

The vulture flew over the sea to the little island.

The man hit him with a coconut.
The vulture flew back with a rotten headache and
retired to the mountains.

The king was very angry. He summoned
his cousin the pole vaulter.
"You are the man to win the island," he said.
"After all, you *are* family."
The king's cousin did a record-
breaking pole vault and nearly
made a perfect landing on
the little island.

But the man hit the pole with a coconut.
The king's cousin floated back holding onto the
broken bit and decided to become a hermit.

The king flew into a towering rage. He called for his secret weapon.

"Cook!" he hollered. "Take him your soggy succotash. That will do the trick."

The cook was halfway to the little
island when the man hit the
succotash with a coconut.
The cook went back to the
palace and packed
her bags.

The greedy king looked all about him. He had lost his champion Olympic swimmer, his head gardener, his pet vulture, his cousin the pole vaulter, and even the palace cook.

"I'd like to come over and talk peace,"
shouted the king.

The man smiled and
beckoned him across.

"You put up a good fight,"
 said the king.
"Yes," said the man.
"Have some coconut."
 And they ate the last one
 from the tree.

"He seems a nice fellow," said the king to the queen.

"I won't take his island after all."

"Because he's a nice fellow?" asked the queen.

"No," said the king. "Because he hasn't got any more coconuts."